# Chef

D0453102

Copyright © QED Publishing 2009

First published in the UK in 2009 by
QED Publishing
A Quarto Group company
226 City Road
London EC1V 2TT
www.qed-publishing.co.uk

All rights reserved. No part of this publication
may be reproduced, stored in a retrieval system,
or transmitted in any form or by any means,
electronic, mechanical, photocopying, recording,
or otherwise, without the prior permission of the
publisher, nor be otherwise circulated in any form
of binding or cover other than that in which it
is published and without a similar condition being
imposed on the subsequent purchaser.

A catalogue record for this book is available from
the British Library.

ISBN 978 1 84835 251 3

Printed and bound in China

**Author** Amanda Askew
**Designer and Illustrator** Andrew Crowson
**Consultants** Shirley Bickler and Tracey Dils

**Publisher** Steve Evans
**Creative Director** Zeta Davies
**Managing Editor** Amanda Askew

Words in bold are
explained in the
glossary on page 24.

# Chef

Amanda Askew
Andrew Crowson

QED
QED Publishing

Meet Rory. He's a chef. He cooks food for people at Rory's Diner.

4

Rory arrives at the **restaurant** at 9 o'clock. The kitchen workers are there to help him to **prepare** the food for lunch.

First, Rory goes over the menu.

"Today, we'll cook leek and potato soup, lamb chops with mint gravy, and chocolate fudge cake."

"Josh, chop the vegetables for the soup. Alice, mix the chocolate cake. Greg, prepare the mint gravy and the mashed potato swirls."

Josh, Greg and Alice start working.

Alice gets the 'Chocolate Delight' recipe book.

Josh starts to chop the leeks and peel the potatoes.

Greg picks fresh
mint from the
herb garden.

Alice
starts to
collect her
**ingredients.**

"Oh no!
The fridge
has broken
down! All
the food
is ruined!"
she shouts.

Rory rushes over to the fridge.

The milk, butter and cheese can't be used. The stock for the gravy will have to be thrown away. The lamb chops will have to be replaced.

Rory phones Farmer John. "We've got an emergency. The fridge is broken. We need milk, butter, cheese and lamb chops – they were today's special."

14

"I have everything, except lamb chops. Will chicken be ok?"

"Yes, that's fine. I'll serve chicken with mushrooms instead," says Rory.

Farmer John delivers
the new food.

Rory and the team work hard to get everything ready for lunchtime.

People start to arrive
at the restaurant at
12 o'clock.

"Three chicken dishes to table 5 please, Freda," Rory says.

By 2 o'clock, most people are eating their desserts. Rory goes into the **dining area** to meet some of the customers. He likes to see that everyone is happy with their food.

"That was the tastiest chicken I've ever eaten. Thank you very much!" one man tells Rory.

"I'm glad to hear it!" Rory smiles.

# Glossary

**Dining area** A place where people eat food at a table.

**Herb** A small plant that can be added to food.

**Ingredient** One of the foods that is used to make a meal.

**Menu** A list of meals served in a restaurant.

**Recipe** A list telling you how to cook a meal or type of food.

**Restaurant** A place where you can buy and eat a meal cooked by a chef.

**Prepare** To get something ready or make something.